W9-CJQ-366

THE ADVENTURES OF ANGUS McGREGOR SERIES

The Rescue

By James Cochrane
Illustrations by Sharon Heim

THE ADVENTURES OF ANGUS McGREGOR SERIES

The Rescue

A charming story about a Scotsman who encounters an injured bear in the woods one day, only to discover that he has the gift of communicating with animals.

Written and told by James Cochrane

Illustrated by Sharon Heim

Magic Lantern Books

Published by Magic Lantern Books
1117 High Vista Drive
Arden, North Carolina 28704
(828) 891-7880

Library of Congress Control Number: 2001092001

ISBN 0-9711001-4-4

Printed in Hong Kong

First Edition

Sold with companion CD

Dedicated to my dear mother, Gwen

Special appreciation to
Barbara Moss, Doug Heim and Doug Rubel
for all of your kind help and support.

On his way home through the woods after fishing one day, Angus McGregor smiles to himself as he thinks about the fish that he has just caught. Mmmm... How tasty it will be for his supper!

A bright red bird is singing happily on a nearby tree branch. Angus looks up and says, “You’re looking mighty cheerful today little fella!”

Suddenly, Angus hears the splintering of wood, then a loud thud! Growls of anguish and pain echo throughout the forest.

"What on earth is that," wonders Angus, before rushing off into the woods to where the noise is coming from.

There he sees a big tree that has fallen to the ground, and beneath the tree, laying flat on his back, is a great big bear with his right leg trapped beneath one of the tree limbs. The bear sits up and struggles to lift the limb from his leg, but the limb, still attached to the tree, is far too heavy for him to lift. The bear lays back down, groaning in despair.

Angus cautiously approaches. He doesn't want to scare the injured bear, then he steps on a twig… "Grrrr!" growls the bear.

"It's okay big fella, I'm not going to hurt you. I just came to help," whispers Angus. Angus and the bear stare at each other for a few moments. Then Angus moves closer, almost on tiptoes, to inspect the damage. "It doesn't look too good," Angus remarks. The nervous bear moans in agreement.

"Listen, I've got a saw that will take care of this mess. I'll have you out of here in a jiffy," says Angus.

The bear frowns and looks worried.

As Angus hurries off, he tells the bear, "Just stay there. I'll be right back."

The bear mutters with a deep sigh, "It doesn't look like I'll be going anywhere."

Angus returns with his chainsaw and a small case with a cross on the side of it.

The chainsaw roars to life, and Angus begins the delicate task of removing the tree limb, piece by piece.

The bear is far too nervous to watch and covers his eyes with his big paw.

Soon the limb is in small pieces, and the bear's leg is free at last.

Angus inspects the bear's wound. "I don't think it's broken, just a bad gash. We'll have to clean it though," Angus informs the bear.

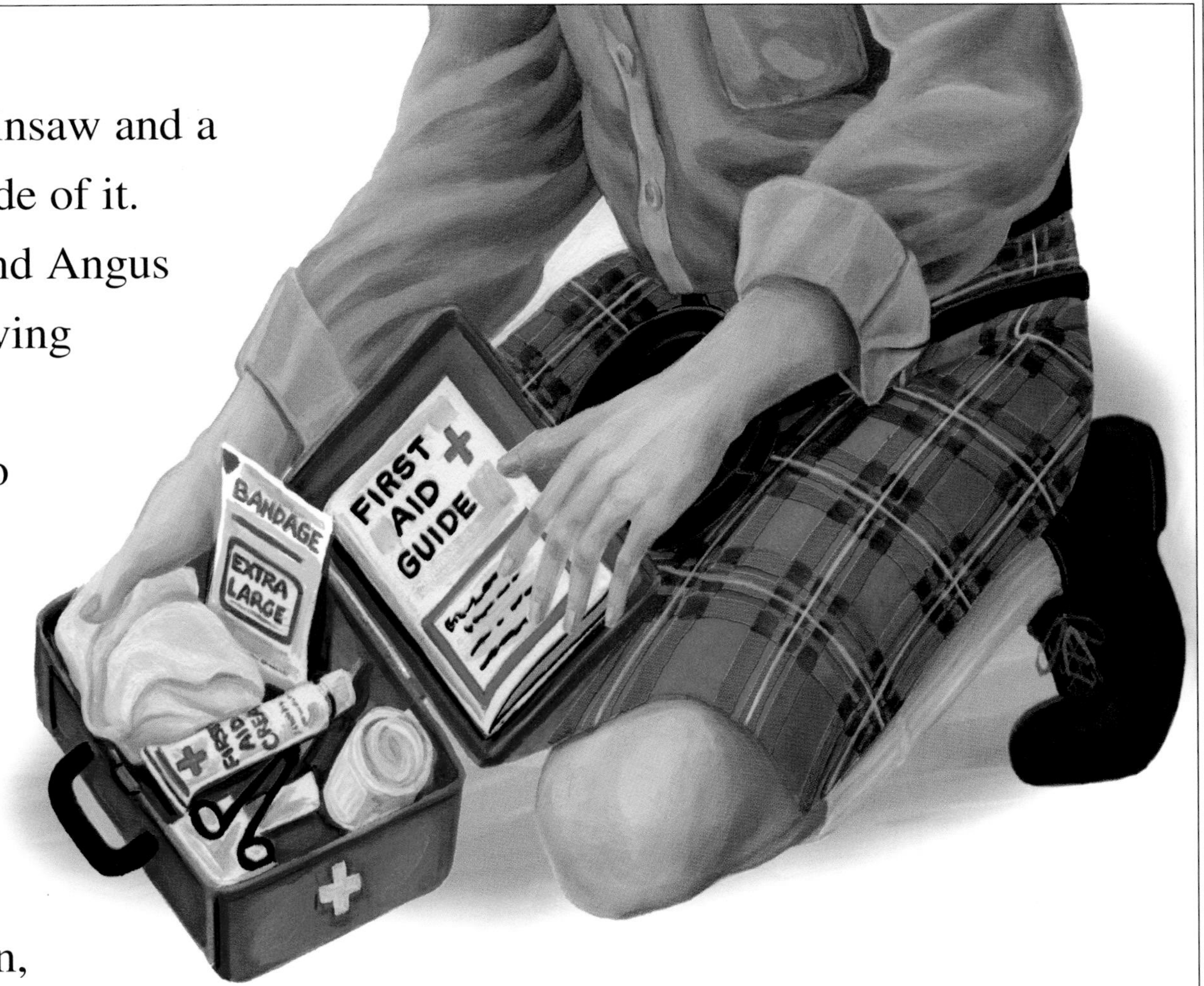

Angus picks up his case with the cross on it, and opens it up in front of the bear, so that the bear can see what is inside. "See, there's nothing in here to be afraid of, just some antiseptic and bandages," assures Angus.

FIRST AID
BANDAGE
EXTRA LARGE
STERILE

Angus takes out a bottle of cleaning alcohol from under a cloth, and applies a generous amount onto the cloth. The fumes from the alcohol are strong, causing Angus's eyes to water.

Just as he is about to apply the cloth to the bear's leg, the nervous bear asks, "Is it going to hurt?"

"No, not really," replies Angus. Then he says, "Phew! I think these fumes are going to my head, I could have sworn you just spoke."

"I did, I'm really worried about my injured leg," replies the bear.

Angus now realizes that he is having a conversation with the bear and begins to stutter, “B-but, but bears can’t talk!”

The bear looks into Angus's eyes and tells him, "All animals can talk. You just have to take the time and listen."

Angus is confused, and asks, "I do?"

"You do," says the bear.

"For instance"...

When you whistle up a song to a bird
He understands every word
Though it may sound a little absurd
You can talk with a bird

And if you wanna share a thought with a deer
You only have to be sincere
Things are not always like they appear
You can talk with a deer

'Cause every living creature has a story inside
If you've got the ears to hear
Just keep your mind and your heart open wide
And they'll be coming in loud and clear

So if you have a conversation with a bear
Even though you might consider it rare
He will listen to whatever you share
He's really quite aware

Every living creature has a story inside
If you've got the ears to hear
Just keep your mind and your heart open wide
And they'll be coming in loud and clear

So when you have a conversation with bear
Even though you might consider it rare
He will listen to whatever you share
He's really quite aware...I'm really quite aware

"I'm really quite aware..." then the bear says, "Hmm! A-hum! Now what about my leg, is this stuff going to hurt?" "No, maybe just a little. The worst is already over," assures Angus. As soon as Angus applies the cloth to the wound, the bear screams! "Oooww! It hurts! You said it wouldn't hurt!"

Angus says. "I said it would hurt a little."

"Hurt a little, it's killing me! Take it off! Take it off!" cries the bear.

Angus removes the cloth, "There, all done. Now, you'll have to keep this wound clean. If you don't, gangrene could set in."

"Ganga who?" asks the bear.

"Gangrene," repeats Angus. "It's a real bad infection, and if you get it, you could lose your leg. I'll put a bandage on it and that will help keep the wound clean," informs Angus.

"Is the bandage going to hurt? Now tell me the truth this time!" says the bear.

Angus gently begins to wrap the bandage around the wound.

BANDAGE
EXTRA LARGE
FIRST AID GUIDE

The bear asks, "What on earth are you wearing?"

"It's my kilt," replies Angus.

"Where do you come from?" inquires the bear.

Angus stops wrapping the bandage to reply, "Across the great waters..."

"I know all about the ocean, but where do you come from?" interrupts the bear.

Angus proudly announces, "From the Highlands of Scotland."

"Never heard of it," states the bear.

"Well, I wouldn't have expected you to have heard about it, being a bear," replies Angus.

The bear feels insulted and says, "I beg your pardon. I'll let you know that I have read some books and I am quite knowledgeable about certain facts, but Scotland, never heard of it!" "I don't believe I'm hearing this, it must be a dream," says Angus, pinching himself.

The bear gently taps Angus on the shoulder with his paw and asks, "Excuse me Angus, are you going to finish fixing my wound before that ganga thing sets in, and my leg falls off?" Angus quickly resumes his bandaging.

"Hmmm... Tell me about Scotland, and your kilt," asks the bear.

"Are you going to interrupt me again?" questions Angus.

"I won't interrupt you again," promises the bear.

Angus tells the bear, "The kilts come in all different colors, and depending on which family of people you belong to, determines the colors that you wear. The families are called clans, and the colors of my kilt are from the McGregor clan, because my name is Angus McGregor."

"That's most unusual," says the bear.

"They say that the first time you wear a kilt, you never want to take it off," continues Angus.

"Well you definitely would not catch me in one, that's for sure," says the bear.

Angus laughs at the thought. "I can just see you in one! The newspaper headlines would read, Scottish bear spotted in the mountains," jokes Angus, and he and the bear chuckle at the remark.

“Oh, and I forgot to mention, we have our own style of dancing, called the Highland Fling, and it goes like this!” Angus begins to dance wildly, throwing his arms and legs in the air, and he twirls around in front of the bear. Then he accidently kicks the first aid box.

The bear slaps his cheeks with his big paws and moans, "Oh, my gosh, what's he doing now?" "Isn't this great fun!" shouts Angus. "No, as a matter of fact, I'm feeling rather dizzy! That's quite enough for one day, thank you," says the bear.

"Heh, heh, oh, okay!" says Angus.

Then Angus asks, “Do animals have names?”

“Of course they do,” informs the bear.

“Really, what’s your name?” inquires Angus.

“My name is Henry,” replies the bear.

“Interesting... well, how did this tree fall down on top of you?” Angus asks Henry.

After a few moments, Henry, a little embarrassed, says, “I…I pushed it over.”

Angus is very surprised and asks. “You pushed the tree down on top of yourself?”

“Not exactly, I had a terrible itch, and I was rubbing my back up against the tree to have a good scratch. That’s when it fell over... I just don’t know my own strength sometimes,” admits Henry.

“Wait a minute! If you had leaned against the tree, it would have fallen away, not on top of you,” states Angus, now at the base of the tree. “Woah, the whole back of this tree’s been chewed away!” shouts Angus.

Henry mutters to himself. "Arthur." Then after briefly looking around, he shouts. "Arthur, Arthur, you come out here at once! I know you're hiding here somewhere!"

A few moments later, a nervous little beaver pokes his head out from behind a nearby bush.

"Hi, Henry," squeaks Arthur, waving his paw. "Oh I'm sorry, Henry. I'm really sorry. I was working behind the tree and I didn't see you. I didn't know you were there until I heard you screaming! I thought I'd killed you and I was so afraid that I just ran away and hid behind the bush!"

Arthur stops for a breath, then says, "I'll make it up to you, I promise I will."

Henry now has his say, “Well, you’d better hope that ganga stuff doesn’t set in, because if it does, you’ll be in big trouble. How are you going to make it up to me?” inquires Henry. Arthur begins to rub his ear, then says, “Well, hmm… I know, I know, I know! I’ll catch lots of fish for you. You love fish, and I could keep you with a very good supply.” “For how long?” Henry asks. After thinking about it, Arthur says, “Well, for at least two weeks, two whole weeks!”

“Just two weeks? I’ll be on my back for months,” grumbles Henry, who then rubs his leg near the wound and cries, “Ooww!”

“Okay. Okay! Three weeks then,” offers Arthur.

“Deal!” agrees Henry, who then gets up and limps over to Angus. “Thanks, Angus, you saved my life.” Angus replies, “You’re welcome, Henry.”

“Well, I’ve had a very traumatic day, and I’m famished. Will it be dinner time soon, Arthur?” asks Henry. Arthur nods, “Yes, Henry. I’ll get right on it.” Henry then limps off to rest. “I guess I’d better start fishing, that Henry’s got a BIG appetite,” says Arthur, as he leaves.

Later that evening, sitting in his armchair in front of the stone fireplace, Angus tells his young sons of his adventure that day. Ian, ten years old, and Stuart, just turned seven, are both listening intently to their father's story. The logs burning in the fireplace crackle and pop, while shadows from the flames dance around on the ceiling above. Angus says "…and as I was cutting away the limb with my saw to free the bear's leg, something suddenly touched the back of my head. I could feel the hairs on the back of my neck stand straight up! I thought it might be another bear, because it was something sharp, just like a bear claw. My legs were shaking, and I slowly turned around to see what it was," Ian and Stuart both whisper, "Another bear!"

"And it was only another branch from the tree that I had backed myself into," laughs Angus.

"Phew!" utter the boys, relieved.

Mrs. McGregor remarks, "You're a fine one with your tales, Angus McGregor."

"But it's not a tale. It really happened!" Angus replies. Mrs. McGregor just shakes her head a little and continues with her knitting.

"Then Henry stood up." Angus jumps up, "He must have been about nine feet tall! He came limping over to me." Angus thumps his feet up and down on the floor, pretending to limp. "And he thanked me for saving his life," says Angus, proudly. "Then off he went, disappearing into the woods... Oh, I nearly forgot," continues Angus, "Just before he disappeared, he stopped for a moment to beat on his chest with his big paws." Angus beats on his chest with his fists and begins to roar like a wild bear. Suddenly, there is a loud, "BANG, CRASH!" over by the sideboard.

Stuart is startled and grabs onto his dad's legs with both arms wrapped around them. "What was that, Dad? " Stuart asks, frightened.

"It's only Misty. She's knocked the cookie jar over trying to get into it," informs Ian.

"You can let go of my legs now, Stuart," says Angus. Stuart lets go and gives a sigh of relief, as Misty the cat scampers off.

"Okay boys, time to scrub the ivory," Angus tells the boys.

Mrs. McGregor chirps in, "Yes boys, it's time to go upstairs and brush your teeth. I'll be up in a few moments to tuck you in."

The boys hug their dad good night. "Thanks, dad. That was a great story!" they tell him.

As Angus reaches into the bin for a fresh log for the fire, Mrs. McGregor asks him, "Was that a true story, Angus?"

Angus replies while placing the log on the fire, “What do you think?”

After all... a promise is a promise!